8/05 $13.75

Daddy Calls Me Man

A RICHARD JACKSON BOOK

Daddy Calls Me Man

by ANGELA JOHNSON

paintings by
RHONDA MITCHELL

ORCHARD BOOKS

NEW YORK

Orchard Books, A Grolier Company, 95 Madison Avenue, New York, NY 10016

Manufactured in the United States of America
Printed and bound by Phoenix Color Corp.
Book design by Jennifer Browne

Hardcover 10 9 8 7 6 5 4 3 2
Paperback 10 9 8 7 6 5 4 3

The text of this book is set in 24 point Aldus.
The illustrations are oil paintings on canvas reproduced in full color.

Library of Congress Cataloging-in-Publication Data
Johnson, Angela.
Daddy calls me man / by Angela Johnson ; paintings by Rhonda Mitchell.
p.   cm.
"A Richard Jackson book"—Half t.p.
Summary: Inspired by his family experiences and his parents'
paintings, a young boy creates four poems.
ISBN 0-531-30042-0 (tr.)   ISBN 0-531-07175-8 (pbk.)
[1. Family life—Fiction. 2. Afro-Americans—Fiction. 3. Paintings—Fiction.]
I. Mitchell, Rhonda, ill. II. Title.
PZ7.J629Dah 1997   [E]—dc21   96-53865

To my loving grandmother,
Mattie Bell Floyd
—A.J.

To Him from whom all blessings flow.
Thanks for everything.
—R.M.

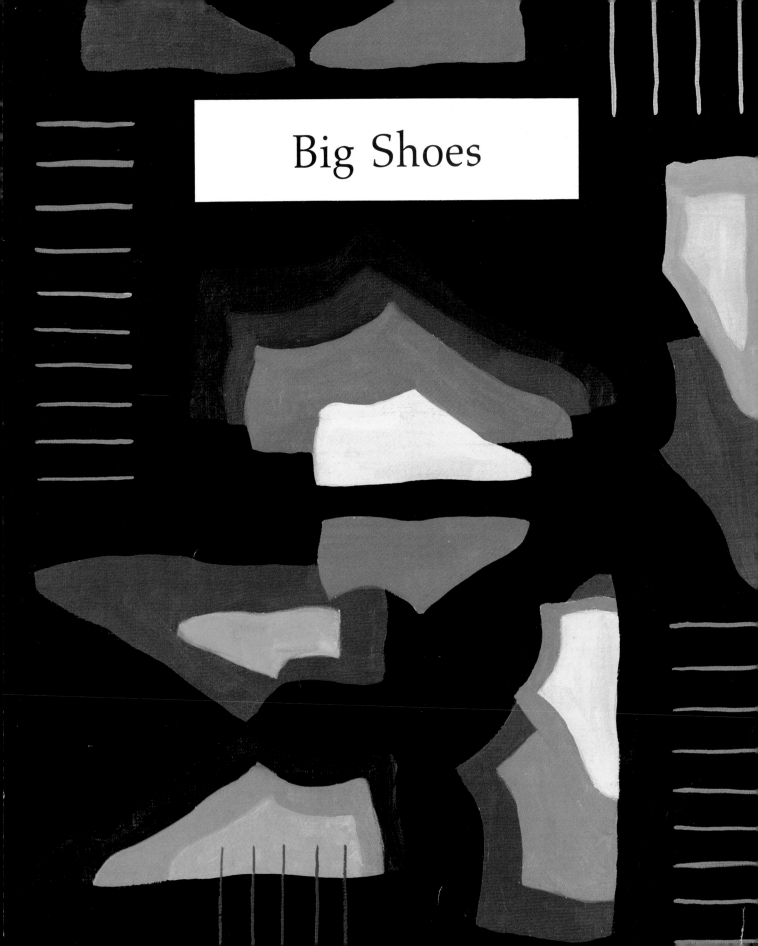

Big Shoes

Tie shoes

Fast shoes

Red and black jump high shoes.

Line them up by Daddy's

and call them all our shoes.

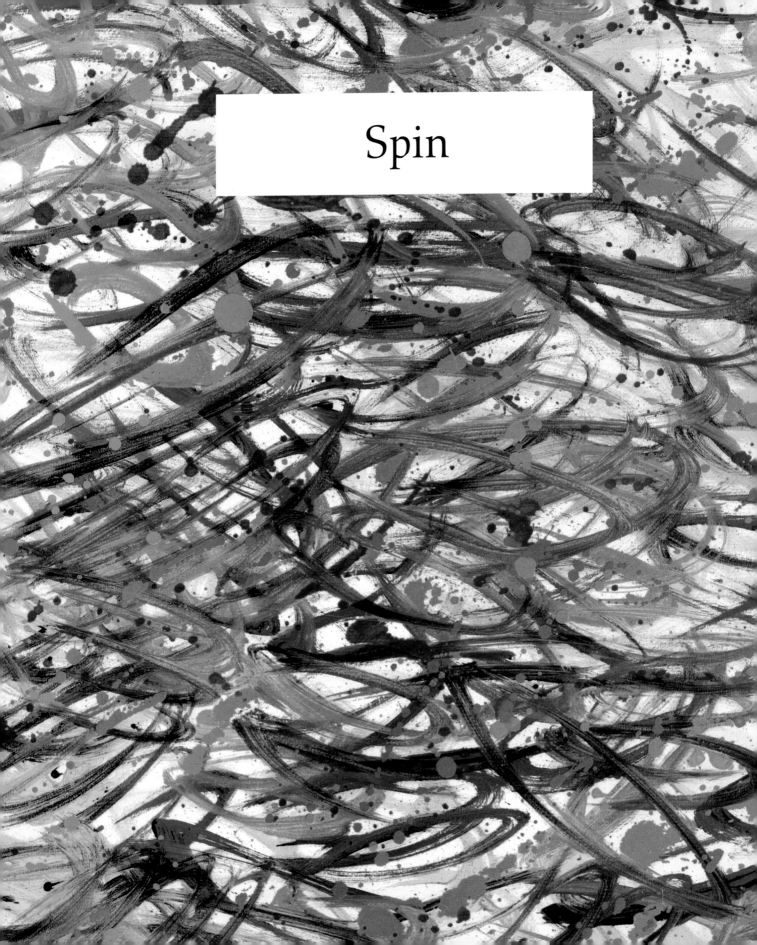

Spin

Spin around the room.

Spin around the tree.

Swirl

Twirl

Spin and twist

Big sister and me.

Noah's Moon

Mama calls it Noah's moon and says
it lives glowing in the sky.

Half a moon
Full moon

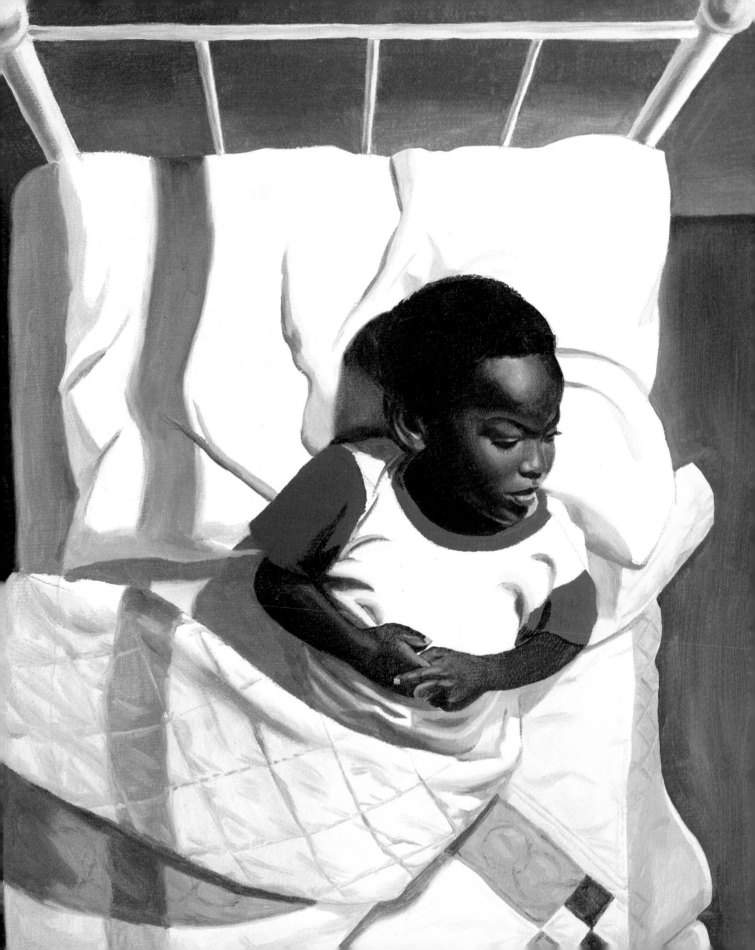

Me asking why.

Full moon, half moon
Glowing in the sky.

Little bitty fingers
and smiles just for me.

I share toys
my room
and JoJo
anytime I can.

Then Mama calls me sweetheart

and Daddy calls me man.